DOWNTOWN DINOSAURS
DINOSAURS OFFSIDE

JEANNE WILLIS

Piccadilly

For Ian Wilcock,
for explaining the Beautiful Game.
J.W.

For Tom and Dan
A. P.

First published in Great Britain in 2014
by Piccadilly Press,
A Templar/Bonnier publishing company
Deepdene Lodge, Deepdene Avenue,
Dorking, Surrey, RH5 4AT
www.piccadillypress.co.uk

A catalogue record for this book is available
from the British Library

ISBN: 978 1 84812 362 5

1 3 5 7 9 10 8 6 4 2

Printed in the UK by CPI (UK) Group, Croydon

CHAPTER 1

KICK-OFF

It was the World Cup. The Uptown Dinosaurs were gripped with football fever, and none more so than the stegosaurs in Fossil Street. Darwin, Uncle Loops and Mr Stigson had been glued to the television since kick-off. That afternoon, all three of them were squashed together on the sofa, watching a thrilling match between Mammals United and Neanderthal Nomads. The goalkeeper had just been savaged by a sabre-toothed tiger, the referee was shilly-

shallying about sending it off and, in the middle of all the drama, the doorbell rang.

'Somebody answer that, please,' said Mrs Stigson, struggling with the wet washing.

'Answer what?' said Uncle Loops. 'I didn't hear anything. Did you, Damian?'

'No,' said Darwin.

It was a total lie. While Uncle Loops had gone a bit deaf and doolally in his old age, there was nothing wrong with Darwin's hearing at all.

BING BONG! There it went again.

'Doorbell, Dad,' Darwin said, giving his father a nudge in the ribs.

Mr Stigson got halfway out of his seat then sat down again.

'Put your glasses on, you silly old fool!' he yelled, waving his fist at the screen.

Uncle Loops rummaged for his spectacles and, in his haste, he put them on upside down. Darwin turned them round the right way for him.

'Dad was talking to the referee, not you, Uncle.'

'Stupid ref!' shouted Mr Stigson. 'Fancy giving the job to a micropachycephalosaurus. Everyone knows the name means small, thick-headed lizard.'

'Even me!' said Uncle Loops. 'I never forget a name, Malcolm.'

'My name is *Maurice*,' said Mr Stigson wearily.

'Mine's Augustus,' said Loops, shaking him by the hand. 'Pleased to meet you.'

BING BONG!

'I'll answer it then, shall I?' tutted Mrs Stigson, striding towards the front door. Before she opened it, she had a quick peek through the letterbox to make sure it wasn't a deadly T. Rex from Downtown – they'd been terrorising the neighbourhood for years.

'Is it a carnivore or a herbibore?' called Uncle Loops.

'Don't you mean herbi*vore*?' said Darwin.

'I meant what I said,' groaned Uncle Loops.

It was the triceratops from Number 27 – the world famous actor, Sir Stratford Tempest, who not only ate herbs but was also extremely boring. He flounced in, blowing his vuvuzela and dragging a trolley full of bottles.

'Get the corkscrew, Maurice,' he trilled. 'Now then, who would like to try some of my delicious pea and ginger beer? It's home-made. The peas are from my allotment.'

'Not for me, thanks,' said Darwin. 'I'm underage.'

'I'd better not either,' shuddered Mr Stigson. 'I can still remember how awful I felt the last time I drank it.'

'I can't,' said Loops. 'Pour me a drop and remind me, Sir Compost.'

Sir Tempest filled a glass to the brim and held it up to the light to admire the colour.

'It certainly looks like pea!' he said proudly.

Loops snatched the glass, took a large swig and pulled a face.

'And it *tastes* like pee,' he said. 'Never mind, it's better than nothing.'

The triceratops squeezed in between Mr Stigson and Uncle Loops and helped himself to some nuts.

'This is cosy, isn't it?' he said, grabbing the remote and changing the channel.

Mr Stigson waved his arms in agitation. 'What are you doing? We're trying to watch the game, Stratford!'

'I'm starring in an advert for underpants,' said Sir Tempest. 'I thought you might like to see them.'

Uncle Loops covered his eyes with a cushion.

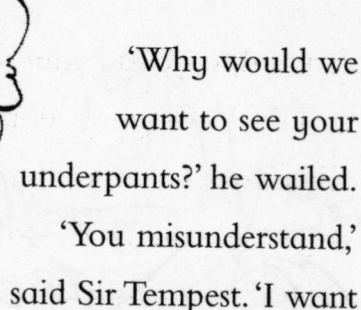

'Why would we want to see your underpants?' he wailed.

'You misunderstand,' said Sir Tempest. 'I want you to see the advert. It'll be on any second.'

'That's a relief,' said Uncle Loops.

'No, it isn't,' said Mr Stigson, snatching the remote and switching back to the sports channel. 'See? Now we've missed a goal!'

'Well, pardon me for breathing,' sulked the triceratops. He turned his back on Mr Stigson to look at Darwin. 'How's school, Darwin?'

Darwin didn't want to talk about school. He didn't want to talk at all – he just wanted to watch the match in peace. However, apart from the chattering, it was hard to see past Sir Tempest's enormous head.

'School's fine, thanks,' he said, craning

forward to get a better view.

'Did I tell you about the time I played a school teacher in a film?' said Sir Tempest, as if anybody cared. 'It was called *Goodbye, Mr Chops* . . . It was a very meaty role.'

Uncle Loops rubbed his stomach hungrily.

'I'd like a roll,' he said. 'But not a meaty one – I'd rather have egg.'

'I'm heating some snacks in the oven,' said Mrs Stigson. 'They're almost ready. What are the odds Phyllis from next door turns up the minute I bring in the food?'

Sure enough, the second she brought the tray in, Mrs Merrick the mastodon put her enormous trunk through the open front window.

'If that's Fat Phyllis, tell her we're not in!' shouted Uncle Loops.

'I heard that, Augustus!' said Mrs Merrick, sniffing the air. 'My sense of hearing is as good

as my sense of smell, and *you* need a bath . . .
Are those freshly baked spring rolls, Lydia?'

Mrs Stigson nodded. 'Would you like one?'

'No – I'd like six, please,' said Mrs Merrick, as
she let herself in. 'After all, I just found your
daughter sobbing outside. She said a monster
stole her dolly. I've brought her back in my
handbag – she's far too young to be playing in
the street on her own.'

She snapped open the bag and Darwin's little
sister, Shelly, popped her head out.

Mrs Stigson gasped. 'I thought she was in the
back garden!'

She picked the little stegosaur up and
comforted her.

'How many times have I told you not to play
out the front?' she said. 'It's too dangerous. Your
brother Livingstone did that and he got eaten
by a gangster T. Rex.'

At the mention of a T. Rex, Shelly burst into tears again. Having already lost a brother, Darwin was very protective of his sister and looked up in alarm.

'Maybe Flint Beastwood's back,' he said.

Darwin had already had several run-ins with the evil tyrannosaurus rex. Only recently, Flint had kidnapped him, trashed their house, stolen the gold watch Uncle Loops got for his one hundred and nintieth birthday, almost killed his friend Dippy and stolen his mother's egg. He would stop at nothing, and now it looked as if he was picking on his kid sister.

'Shelly, what did the monster who took your doll look like?' he said. 'Was he taller than Dad, with tiny arms and piggy eyes?' 'Did he have bad breath and a silly hat?' added Sir Tempest.

The little stegosaur shook her head and made gestures to show that whoever did it was a bit taller than Darwin and a whole lot uglier.

'It was probably Ozzi,' said Mrs Merrick, taking the last spring roll. 'That austra-lopithecus is a wicked little thief. You know he's stolen your wheels, Maurice?'

Mr Stigson ran over to the window and gazed in horror at his new car – not a single tyre remained.

'The little monkey!' he said.

'Ozzi's worse than a monkey,' said Sir Tempest. 'He's almost human. I dread to think what he'll get up to when he evolves.'

Uncle Loops turned the telly up to its full volume.

'I can't hear the football!' he complained.

'Put your hearing aid in!' said Mrs Stigson, clapping her hands over her ears.

'Eh?' said Uncle Loops.

By now, Darwin had given up trying to watch the match – it was impossible with all the noise going on – but he'd always dreamt of being a professional footballer. Spurred on by the matches he'd seen so far, he decided to go to the playground in No Man's Land and practise his skills with his friends, the ankylosaur twins.

'Mum, I'm going to play footy with Frank and Ernest,' he said.

'Take Shelly with you, dear,' Mrs Stigson replied. 'I need to fumigate Uncle Loops's bedroom. Just don't let her fall in the pond.'

But, as it turned out, Shelly falling in the pond was the least of Darwin's worries.

CHAPTER 2

MAN ON!

Darwin found his football, put it in the pushchair with Shelly, and wheeled her round to Frank and Ernest's house at the corner of Fossil Street. He'd known the twins since he went to nursery – they looked so similar, even their own mother struggled to tell them apart. This was great for playing practical jokes on the teachers, but there was no fooling Darwin . . . or was there?

He knocked on their door and they ran into the hall, fencing with cucumbers.

'Hey, Frank,' said Darwin. 'Fancy doing some football practice?'

'I'm Ernest,' said Frank.

'I'm Frank,' said Ernest.

Darwin looked them up and down. It really was impossible to tell who was who, but it didn't matter. They were equally good fun.

'Whoever,' he said. 'Can you come out to play?'

The ankylosaurs didn't need asking twice. They were very keen on sport and had won several cups and medals. One of them was captain of the school football team, but whether it was Frank or Ernest, nobody knew for sure.

It was no great distance to the playground. When they arrived, it was full of little herbivores and primitive, furry mammals playing on the swings and slides. There were plenty of parents around, many of whom were big brachiosaurs, so it felt quite safe.

Unfortunately, there were already two ragged-looking teams of teenage megalotheriums larking about on the official pitch, and Darwin didn't like to ask if they could join in. He recognised them from the bus stop and could tell by all the swearing that they went to the Academy for Delinquent Omnivores near Raptor Road.

'Let's make our own pitch, over by the Primeval Forest,' said Frank – or possibly Ernest.

'It's too crowded here,' said Ernest – or possibly Frank.

Darwin hesitated. The Primeval Forest was one of those places parents always warned their children about. It was dark and dangerous, especially for young herbivores. It was okay on the outskirts, but towards the middle there were swamps and quicksand and, during the breeding season, it became a hunting ground for carnivores. He'd got into serious trouble there on several occasions and right now he had Shelly to look after.

'You're not scared, are you?' said Frank.

'No, Ernest,' said Darwin. 'It's not like we're going deep into the forest. No carnivore in his right mind would attack us near the edge, not with all these grown-ups about.'

'Ah, but what if the carnivore *wasn't* in his right mind?' said Ernest.

'Don't be such a wuss, Frank,' said Darwin although, secretly, he was a bit worried himself.

He set off with the pushchair over the bumpy

field towards the trees, parked Shelly where he could keep an eye on her and helped Frank and Ernest mark out the goal with their jackets.

After doing keepy-uppies for a while, they decided to practise taking penalty shots.

Being a stegosaur, evolution hadn't given Darwin the best goalie hands in the dinosaur kingdom, but he had a solid skull and was good at headers. He let the first two goals in but when Frank belted the ball towards him the

third time, he did a running jump, caught it mid-flight and nutted it so hard it almost went into the forest.

Unfortunately, that was the moment when Ozzi's pet cynognathus ran out of the forest and, being a prehistoric dog, chased the ball and grabbed it in his enormous jaws. 'Drop it, Nogs!' commanded Darwin in the tone he usually saved for Uncle Loops.

Sadly, Nogs hadn't been to puppy classes and, with a wicked glint in his eye, he tossed the ball in the air, caught it in his mouth and punctured it with his razor-sharp fangs. There was a pop, a loud hiss and it went as flat as a cowpat.

'Maybe I could blow it up,' said Darwin.

At which point Nogs cocked his leg and sprayed the dead ball with a stream of amber wee.

'Rather you than me,' said Frank.

'Have you got another ball at home, Darwin?' asked Ernest.

He did have, but he'd kicked it over the fence and damaged Mrs Merrick's pansies, so she wouldn't give it back.

'Haven't you got one?' he asked the twins.

They shook their heads.

'Not any more. Kicked them all over the fence,' said Frank.

'Mrs Merrick's?' sighed Darwin.

The twins nodded. There was no chance of anyone getting their ball back, then. The game was ruined. But just as they were about to go home, Ozzi appeared from behind them.

'Man on!' said Frank.

No Man's Land was australopithecus territory, so it was no surprise to see him. But, to their joy, he was posing with his foot on a football. Although he only spoke in grunts, it was quite clear that he was offering to sell it to them.

'How much?' asked Darwin.

Ozzi held up two fingers. It was hard to tell whether he was making a rude gesture or showing them the asking price of the ball but,

guessing he wanted two pounds for it, they rooted through their belongings for some loose change. Darwin handed the coins over to Ozzi, who grabbed them with a hideous snicker, shoved them somewhere in his filthy fur and ran jingling back to the forest.

'Play on!' said Darwin. 'Get in goal, Frank. My turn to take a kick.'

Rather than pick the new ball up and place it near the goal, in his excitement Darwin decided to kick it back onto the pitch from where it lay.

'Ready, Frank?' he said.

'Yep!' said Ernest.

Darwin charged towards the ball, swung his foot back and booted it as hard as he could. Then, with a painful yell, he collapsed onto the grass, clutching his foot and rolling about in agony. The twins came running over.

'What's happened – did you fall?' asked Ernest.

Darwin sat up and rubbed his stubbed toe.

'I fell for Ozzi's trick!' he groaned. 'That football's fake. It's made from solid rock.'

Frank crouched down and examined it. 'You're right – it's a boulder painted to look like leather. It's even got a logo.'

'Why does Ozzi keep picking on us?' said Darwin, remembering all the practical jokes that the australopithecus had played on him in the past. He'd swapped his swimming trunks when Darwin was taking part in the Dinosaur Olympics; he'd switched signposts and led all the competitors into a swamp; he'd changed the wheels on Darwin's bike for square ones, and that wasn't the half of it.

'I've had enough,' said Darwin.

But there was more to come. Shelly let out a shriek and as Darwin whipped round, he saw a T. Rex coming towards them. It wasn't big and it wasn't clever but, nevertheless, it was a carnivore and it wasn't to be trusted.

'He's got a football,' whispered Ernest.

'A real one,' said Frank eagerly.

'Even so . . .' Darwin frowned, standing in front of the pushchair to protect his sister. 'I don't like the look of him.'

'That's a bit rexist, isn't it?' said Frank.

'He can't help the way he looks,' said Ernest. 'He's just a kid like us.'

Darwin wasn't convinced he was anything like them at all – his teeth were a lot sharper, he kept licking his lips and he had a horribly

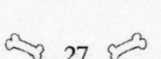

familiar look about him.

'Can I play?' said Rocky Beastwood.

Up close Darwin realised it was Flint's nephew!

'No,' said Darwin.

By now, Shelly was screaming and pointing at the junior tyrannosaurus. Although she couldn't talk yet, Darwin guessed that he was the monster who had snatched her doll.

'Why can't I play?' said Rocky.

Frank and Ernest took Darwin to one side.

'Don't upset him,' said Frank.

'He might turn nasty,' said Ernest.

'He's already nasty,' said Darwin.

But they had a point, so he tried to let Rocky down gently.

'You can't play because . . . I have to go to the dentist right now,' said Darwin.

Rocky Beastwood looked at him sideways and made a fist.

'You *will* have to go to the dentist if you
don't let me play,' he said.

'We have piano lessons,' said Frank and
Ernest, grabbing their jackets. 'Oh look, there's
our enormously fierce dad coming over to
collect us . . . Yoo-hoo, Father!'

As the three of them ran to the safety of the
playground with the pushchair, Rocky

Beastwood looked in vain for the ankylosaurs' fierce father. He wasn't the brightest carnivore in the cave and when he realised the twins' dad had never been there in the first place, he threw back his head and roared.

'Why don't you *like* me? You're mean! I'm tellin' Uncle Flint about you!'

It was the last thing any herbivore wanted to hear, least of all Darwin.

CHAPTER 3

BAD HEADER

As Darwin limped indoors with the pushchair, there was a nasty atmosphere in the room and, for once, it wasn't because Uncle Loops had been eating beans. All the lights were out and Mr Stigson was glaring at the blank screen on the TV.

'What's for dinner, Mum?' said Darwin.

Mrs Stigson appeared with a raw carrot in her hand.

'It was going to be vegetable curry, but the oven isn't working.'

'Good!' said Uncle Loops. 'The last time I ate curry, I had to rush to the toilet ten times and, believe me, that's not easy in a stair-lift.'

Darwin gave Shelly back to his mother and sat next to his father and uncle on the sofa.

'Why aren't you watching the game?' he asked. 'I know Woolly Mammoth Wanderers are bottom of the league but they're going to slaughter Coelacanth City.'

'There's a power cut, dear boy,' said Sir Tempest. 'It happened right in the middle of the game. Maurice is furious, aren't you, Maurice?'

Mr Stigson didn't look very happy at all.

'Mammoths were ten–nil up,' he grumbled.

'Now I'll never know who won.'

'I may not know much about the offside rule,' snorted Mrs Merrick, 'but considering most of the Coelacanths were trampled flat by halftime, if they win I'll eat my hat.'

'You might have to,' said Mrs Stigson. 'I'm not sure there's enough salad to go round if you're staying for dinner.'

Darwin sighed. He'd been looking forward

to a hot supper. But as they sat around the table eating salad in the dark, things were about to get even more depressing.

'I can't see a thing,' complained Mrs Merrick. 'I almost ate my napkin.'

'You're chewing my tie, Phyllis!' complained Sir Tempest, snatching it away from her molars. 'Haven't you got any candles, Lydia?'

Mrs Stigson shook her head. 'Sorry, I used them all up on Uncle Loops's birthday cake.'

'I remember it as if it was yesterday,' said Uncle Loops as he cut up his place mat. 'I was ninety, wasn't I, Douglas?'

'A hundred and ninety,' said Darwin.

'That's nothing,' said Uncle Loops. 'My father lived to be two hundred and fifty and he still had all his own hair.'

'Nonsense!' said Mrs Merrick. 'Stegosaurs don't have hair.'

'I never said he was a stegosaurus,' said Uncle Loops. 'Mother was a bit of a gal.'

'Was she in the theatre?' asked Sir Tempest.

Uncle Loops was just about to answer when a football-sized rock smashed through the front window, hit him on the head and knocked him out cold.

'Uncle, are you all right?' cried Darwin, lifting Loops's head out of the salad bowl.

'Woe, woe and thrice woe!' cried Sir Tempest, wringing his hooves. 'Alas, dear Augustus Loops lies dead! Such a cruel blow, such a tragic waste!'

Mrs Merrick slapped him round the face with her trunk.

'You're hysterical, Stratford,' she said. 'Calm down and let me see the patient. I'm trained in first aid. I agree he looks dead, but then he often does. Help me get him on the rug so I can put him in the recovery position.'

'Is it safe to move him?' said Mrs Stigson as they wrestled Uncle Loops to the floor. 'What if he has a brain injury?'

'How will we ever know, Lydia?' said Mrs Merrick.

Uncle Loops wasn't moving. He lay there with his eyes shut and his false teeth hanging out.

'Is he breathing?' said Darwin.

'Hard to tell at his age,' said Mrs Merrick, whipping out his dentures. 'I'll give him the kiss of life just to be on the safe side.'

'That'll finish him off,' muttered Sir Tempest as she knelt astride Uncle Loops. She was just about to give him mouth-to-mouth when he sat up.

'Hot the whipping fleck are do you-ing, Fart Frillies?' he shrieked.

'Oh no! His speech is all confused,' said Mrs Stigson.

'No change there, then,' said Sir Tempest.

Mrs Merrick pinned the struggling patient back down with her tusks.

'Keep still, Augustus! I'm trying to resuscitate you.'

'Geroff!' he squirmed. 'I'm a mappily harried flan!'

Somehow, Uncle Loops wriggled out from underneath her and tried to pull himself up on his walking frame. He'd been wobbly on his feet for years, but now he couldn't even get up. It didn't help that the brakes were off and, as the frame shot out from under him and dragged him across the rug, he spouted even more nonsense than usual.

'Rippery slug!' he said, as his foot gave way.
'Bake me up to ted, bumsody!'

Darwin tried to help him up, but Uncle
Loops's sense of balance had gone completely.

'Let's take him to hospital,' said Mrs Stigson.
'Help me get him into the car, Maurice.'

'It's got no wheels, dear,' said Mr Stigson.
'Ozzi stole them, remember? And I bet he threw
that rock through our window.'

'Me too,' said Darwin. Right now, he was filled with hatred for the australopithecus. Usually, he was just annoying, but he'd almost killed Uncle Loops – he might never be able to walk again.

'I'm going to report Ozzi to the police,' said Mr Stigson. 'Don't worry, Loops, we'll get you to hospital somehow.'

'How?' said Mrs Stigson. 'Our car's out of action, Mrs Merrick only has a tricycle and, as far as I know, Sir Tempest doesn't drive.'

'I don't need to. I'm a famous actor, darling,' said the triceratops. 'Larry, my chauffeur, takes me everywhere in his limousine.'

'Do you think he'd do us a favour and give Uncle Loops a lift to A and E?' asked Mrs Stigson.

Sir Tempest pursed his lips.

'I'm afraid Larry is resting at the moment,' he said, lowering his voice to a stage whisper.

'Banned from driving. Please don't press me for details, but he took out a meat wagon, two trucks and a nun, and went off the end of the pier.'

Mr Stigson paced up and down in his slippers and tried to think of something.

'Mind the broken glass!' fretted Mrs Stigson. 'I don't want to visit you in hospital too.'

'Got it!' he said, gazing out into the garden. 'We'll take Loops in my wheelbarrow.'

'Your *wheelbarrow*?' exclaimed Mrs Stigson. 'But it's full of manure!'

'I'll tip it on the rhubarb and give it a rinse,' said Mr Stigson. 'What choice do we have?'

There wasn't one, so while Mr Stigson got his hose out, Mrs Stigson fetched pillows and blankets and, with Darwin's help, they bundled Uncle Loops into the wheelbarrow and tried to make him as comfortable as possible.

'This isn't as lumfortable as it cooks!'

gibbered Uncle Loops. 'Bind the mumps!'

'Try not to talk,' said Mrs Merrick.

'Will it strain his brain?' worried Mrs Stigson, grabbing the handles.

'No,' said Mrs Merrick, 'he's just annoying me.'

Darwin stood on the front step, not sure what to do for the best.

'Can I go with him, Mum?' he asked.

Before she could answer, Mrs Merrick started bossing everyone about.

'No, Darwin, you stay at home and look after Shelly,' she said. 'Your mother and I will accompany your uncle to hospital because your father will only get in the way.'

'No, I won't!' insisted Mr Stigson.

'You will, Maurice,' said Sir Tempest. 'You will.'

Mrs Merrick tucked Uncle Loops back under his blankets and gave the triceratops a cold stare.

'Go home, Stratford,' she said. 'You're not helping. Maurice, run and report Ozzi and, on the way back, call into the glazier and tell him to come and fix your window. It's going to rain.'

'I'm ringing in the sane,' sang Uncle Loops,

'just ringing in the sane! What a funderful wheeling, I'm haaappy again!'

'I'm glad one of us is,' snapped Mrs Merrick. 'I'm missing dinner because of you.'

Darwin waved goodbye as Mrs Merrick and his mother wheeled Uncle Loops to the hospital while his father went to the police station. When they were out of sight, he went back indoors, shut the door and tried to look after his baby sister.

They were home alone.

CHAPTER 4

UNCLE LOOPS SCORES

By the time Mrs Merrick and Mrs Stigson
arrived at the Accident and Emergency
Department with Uncle Loops, it was so busy
there was hardly room to push the
wheelbarrow. To make things worse, Mrs

Merrick wasn't very good at steering and managed to run over a perfectly healthy struthiomimus. He'd only come to visit a sick relative but ended up being admitted with two crushed ribs and a broken toe.

It was a Saturday afternoon and the place was rammed with dinosaurs of all shapes and sizes sporting every injury imaginable – and

some no one could imagine in their wildest dreams. Among others, there was a mosasaur with a loo-brush rammed up his snout, a saltopus with a model ship stuck to his head with superglue, and a ceratosaur with his foot caught in a kettle.

'That's not a pretty sight, is it?' said Mrs Merrick, sneering at a group of middle-aged

megalosaurs hobbling about in muddy football kits. By the looks of it, they'd been for a kick-about in the park after years of lounging about on the sofa and were now suffering from strained ligaments, palpitations and very unfashionable trainers.

'I blame the World Cup,' said Mrs Stigson. 'Suddenly everyone thinks they can play.'

'Bambiraptor Bounders – four; Becklespinax – nil,' shouted Uncle Loops.

'Quiet, Augustus!' snapped Mrs Merrick. 'If you don't stop spouting football results from five centuries ago, I shall smother you with your own pillow.'

Her impatience was understandable. Uncle Loops had been yelling out the scores since they left home and showed no signs of stopping.

'He can't help it – he's had a blow to the head,' said Mrs Stigson.

'He'll have another one if he doesn't shut up,' said Mrs Merrick.

'Hysilophodons – three; Troodon Troopers – two!' shouted Loops.

Mrs Stigson tried her best to distract him. 'Would you like a biscuit?' she asked.

'Thanks,' said Mrs Merrick, 'I'll have a packet of Jammy Dodgers, a sack of doughnuts and a tin of pink wafers, please – the canteen is over there.'

Mrs Stigson handed Mrs Merrick her purse.

'Actually, I was talking to Loops,' she said, 'but why don't you go and see what they've got while I sit with him? My treat. Would you like a drink, Uncle?'

'Bee and pinger geer,' said Uncle Loops. 'Ceratosaur Conquerors – nil; Iguanodon County – five ...'

As Mrs Merrick charged off to raid the

refreshment counter, the nurse called out Uncle Loops's name and Mrs Stigson wheeled him into a cubicle to be examined. To Mrs Stigson's dismay, the doctor was a dinopithecus and, although he'd only just finished medical school, being a giant baboon he was a terrible know-it-all who actually knew very little.

'I'm Dr Simian,' he said. 'What's the

problem? No, don't tell me. Your son is wedged in a wheelbarrow and you want antibiotics to grease him out.'

'He's not my son,' said Mrs Stigson. 'I'm not that old!'

'You are to me,' said Dr Simian, doodling all over his notes. 'How much does he weigh – sixty bunches of bananas?'

'I don't know,' said Mrs Stigson.

The doctor tapped his pencil on his huge forehead. 'Of course you don't,' he said, scratching his hairy armpits and sniffing his fingers. 'Stegosaur brains are the size of a walnut. I learnt that at medical school. It's pitiful really.'

'It's a pity they didn't teach you any manners,' said Mrs Stigson. 'My uncle is not wedged – he was hit on the head by a boulder.'

'Old Edmontonians – three; Gastonia

Gunners – nil!' giggled Loops. 'Plesiosaur Players – four; Archaeopteryx – two.'

'Hmm,' said Dr Simian, picking his nose. 'The patient has an irritating condition known as Resultus Repetitious. There's no cure – but gagging him might bring some relief.'

Mrs Stigson refused to accept it. 'Maybe it's concussion,' she said. 'He's lost his sense of balance.'

'So prop him up with a washing pole,' the doctor said with a shrug. 'Next!'

But Mrs Stigson wasn't about to be batted aside. 'There must be something more you can do for him,' she said. 'He's always been a little crazy, but nothing like this.'

Dr Simian blew a raspberry, reached into a drawer and pulled out a pair of nutcrackers. 'I could try surgery,' he said. 'But first I need to find his brain.'

'It's in his head,' insisted Mrs Stigson. 'At least, it was this morning.'

'Maybe it is, maybe it isn't,' said Dr Simian, swinging from the light by one arm. 'Get him up and bend him over. I need to examine him.'

'Aren't you going to wash your hands?' said Mrs Stigson.

'Afterwards – I don't want to catch his germs,' he said, jumping down and catapulting Uncle Loops out of the wheelbarrow with his feet.

Just then, Mrs Merrick burst through the curtains with sugar and jam all round her trunk.

'Good heavens! What is poor Augustus doing face down on the lino?' she said.

'I told the doctor he couldn't stand,' explained Mrs Stigson, 'but he ignored me. He says Uncle Loops is suffering from Resultus Repetitious.'

'We're *all* suffering from Resultus Repetitious,' said Mrs Merrick. 'Anyway, there's no such condition, he made it up. Dr Simian, if you don't book this patient in for a brain scan immediately, I'll report you for impersonating a human. Lydia, help me put Loops back into the barrow.'

'Fart Frillies – ten; Dinopithecus – nil,' hooted Uncle Loops as they pushed him down the corridor towards the X-ray department.

'Sometimes it's almost as if he knows exactly what he's talking about,' said Mrs Merrick, but Mrs Stigson's mind was elsewhere.

'I hope Darwin's all right,' she said. 'Shelly can be a bit of a handful sometimes.'

Back at home, Darwin had tried everything to keep his sister amused, but it wasn't working. She'd emptied all the cupboards, poured glue in Uncle Loops's slippers and inserted a cheese cracker in the DVD player.

Right now,
he was busy
trying to scrub
red crayon off
the wall. He'd
given Shelly
plenty of paper
to draw on but
she'd eaten it
and when he
went upstairs
to find her a

jigsaw puzzle, she'd scribbled everywhere. He
was down on his hands and knees with a
scrubbing brush and a bucket of soapy water
when he heard scratching at the front door.

'Shelly, what are you doing now?' he groaned.

But she had fallen asleep under a pile of
cushions – it wasn't her. He stopped what he

was doing and put his ear to the door — *scratch*, *scrabble*, *scratch*. He was wondering what on earth it could be when he heard a familiar whine, followed by a dog-like howl.

'Nogs!' he yelled through the door. 'Go home.'

The cynognathus sat on the doorstep and howled until Darwin couldn't bear it any more. He opened the door, bracing himself to be hit in the face with a custard pie or similar by Ozzi — it

was bound to be a set-up for a practical joke. But nothing happened — there was no sign of the australopithecus at all. That didn't mean he wasn't there, of course — he enjoyed a game of hide and seek as much as the next sub-human — but if he was planning to jump out and surprise his victim, he was taking a very long time. Apart from that, Nogs seemed genuinely upset, as if he'd been abandoned.

Cautiously, Darwin went outside and searched the front garden to see if Ozzi was there or not. He looked behind the garage, under the bushes, he even checked inside the dustbin — Ozzi'd hidden there before and almost given the dustman a heart attack. There was no sign of him now, but when Darwin looked in the flowerbed near the broken window he found something even more horrible among the nasturtiums. It was a massive T. Rex footprint.

It wasn't Ozzi who'd thrown the rock — it must have been Flint Beastwood! The evidence was right in front of his eyes. Darwin shuddered and hurried back indoors.

Keeping a nervous eye out in case Flint suddenly appeared and shoved his hideous, bony head through the broken pane, Darwin called the police.

'I'd like to report an attempted murder,' he said.

The police were so keen to arrest the gangster that, as soon as Darwin mentioned Flint's name, they promised to send someone round to inspect the rogue footprint straight away.

Darwin hid behind the sofa with Shelly in case Beastwood returned and, with his hands over his ears to block out Nog's howls, he waited for the chief detective to arrive.

CHAPTER 5

FANCY FOOTWORK

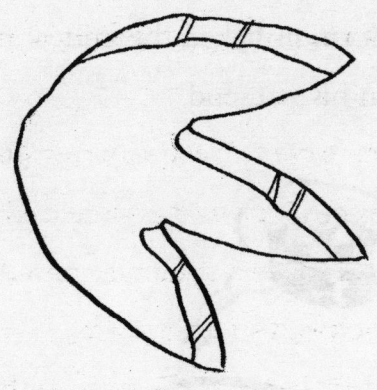

While Darwin was watching the detective make a plaster cast of Flint's footprint, his dad was down at the police station arguing with the constable behind the desk – a rather bored proceratops with one eye.

'I'm telling you, it was an australopithecus who threw that boulder at Uncle Loops,' he insisted.

'Name, sir?' yawned the policeman.

'Maurice,' said Mr Stigson. 'With one R – it's French.'

The policeman licked the end of his pen and scribbled on his notepad.

'One R? Let me get this right,' he muttered. 'The suspect is a French australopithecus called Maurice.'

'No, *I'm* Maurice,' said Mr Stigson.

'The australopithecus is Ozzi. He lives in No Man's Land.'

'Ozzi?' said the policeman. 'That name rings a bell.'

'He's always ringing bells,' groaned Mr Stigson. 'Then he runs away. He's a practical joker, but he's gone too far now. He's a danger to society – I want him arrested!'

The policeman waited for him to stop ranting and finished his struthiomimus-egg sandwich.

'Could you describe him to me, sir?'

Mr Stigson didn't need any prompting.

'Yes – he's a short, fat, hairy menace.'

The policeman whipped out a photo and waved it in his face.

'Is that him, by any chance?'

Mr Stigson recognised Ozzi's nasty, lop-sided little grin immediately and nodded.

'In which case, he never threw that rock,' said

the policeman. 'At the time the alleged incident occurred, he was locked in a cell at this station, having been arrested for carrying offensive weapons.'

Mr Stigson went pale. 'Ozzi had *guns*?'

'No, sir. Two long sticks with rubber carnivore feet stuck onto the ends. As a fellow herbivore I'm sure you find that as offensive as I do.'

Mr Stigson pulled a disgusted face. 'What on earth was he doing with them?'

The policeman picked the cress out of his teeth and shrugged.

'Your guess is as good as mine, sir. We're still holding him for questioning, but if I were to make a guess, I'd say he was laying a false trail of T. Rex prints to put the wind up the good citizens of Uptown.'

'Shocking,' said Mr Stigson.

But if Ozzi hadn't thrown the rock, who had? As if to answer his question, there was a loud commotion outside as a recently-captured suspect struggled to resist arrest. Suddenly the door was booted off its hinges and Mr Stigson ducked behind a chair in terror.

The prisoner was bundled into the station accompanied by two brachiosaurs – one tall

and skinny, one short and chubby – and the
chief detective, who read out the rights.

'Flint Beastwood, you have been arrested for
the attempted murder of Augustus Loops. You
have the right to remain silent, but anything
you do say may be taken down and used in
evidence against you —'

'Shut it, you turnip!' shouted Flint. 'I'm innocent!'

Mr Stigson peered around the chair and noted that the police station was wallpapered with *WANTED* posters of Flint Beastwood and his gang, including Mr Cretaceous the deadly deinosuchus and Terry O'Dactyl the psychotic pteranodon, neither of whom looked the slightest bit innocent.

'Calm down, Mr Beastwood,' said the tall arresting officer as he put handcuffs on him. 'You will have your say in court.'

Scared as he was, Mr Stigson stood up from behind the chair and confronted Flint.

'I hope they throw the book at you!' he said. 'I hope you go to prison for life. Uncle Loops may never walk again.'

Flint fixed him with his beady eyes, which were glowing a violent shade of red.

'Nor will you if I get sent down,' he growled.
'I have friends in very low places, Maurice.
They know where you live.'

'Stop intimidating the witness!' said the
chubby arresting officer, rapping Beastwood on
the snout  with his
truncheon. It
was a silly
thing to do
as it only
enraged him
further. Mr
Stigson had
a ghastly
feeling that
Flint was
about to snap his handcuffs – the chain looked
a bit thin – one quick jerk and he'd be free.

'I'm not a witness!' blurted Mr Stigson. 'I never saw Mr Beastwood anywhere near my house. In fact, I can't imagine why you arrested him.'

'That's more like it, Maurice,' said Flint. 'Keep talking.'

'O-k-kay,' he stammered. 'The reason I came here was to report Ozzi, not Flint – that's true isn't it, constable?'

The policeman behind the desk took a while to reply as he was eating six treacle toffees at once for a bet.

'I'm waiting,' said Flint, tapping his foot. 'Did Stigson grass me up?'

'Mmm? Just a sec . . . toffee stuck,' said the constable. 'Grass you up? Nope.'

For one happy moment, Mr Stigson thought he was off the hook, but Flint was still looking him up and down suspiciously.

'You're squirming, Maurice,' he said. 'Guilty

conscience, perhaps? You say you didn't report me, but *somebody* did. Why else would I be arrested in front of my own wife, dragged out of my club at The Prehysterical and thrown into a police wagon?'

'It wasn't me, I swear on my son's life,' said Mr Stigson.

The minute he said it, he regretted it.

'Ah, your precious son.' Flint grinned. 'Officer, remind me who made the call?'

'Don't tell him, Stan,' said the chubby officer.

'Not telling!' said the skinny one. 'The young stegosaur who made the accusation shall remain nameless for his own protection.'

Flint narrowed his tiny eyes.

'Darwin!' he hissed.

Mr Stigson felt as if he was going to faint.

'It can't have been my boy!' he said. 'Why would he? He has no evidence.'

The detective held up the plaster cast of the print he'd found in the Stigsons' garden.

'I do!' he said, grabbing hold of Flint's ankle to measure his toes against it. 'Exhibit number one – a T. Rex print that matches the prisoner's foot exactly.'

Flint looked confused. 'It can't be mine,' he protested. 'I was nowhere near Fossil Street. I have witnesses.'

The detective smiled. 'They all say that, sir. Where were you exactly at the time the incident happened?'

'I was visiting my old granny in hospital,' grunted Flint.

The detective and the arresting officers fell onto the carpet laughing.

'His old granny!' hooted the chubby one.

'A likely story!' giggled the skinny one. 'Never heard that one before.'

But Flint wasn't laughing. 'It's not funny. She's broken her jaw,' he said. 'She can't chew so I took her some meat paste to suck.'

He sounded so convincing, the detective stopped laughing and stood up again.

'You say you have witnesses?' he said. 'Who are they exactly?'

'Micky Mouse and Donald Duck?' scoffed the arresting officers.

Flint spat and cleared his throat.

'Lydia Stigson and Phyllis Merrick,' he said. 'Augustus Loops is in the same ward as my granny. The witnesses were by his bed at the time of my visit – we exchanged words.'

Mr Stigson guessed they were very rude words. Even so, he leapt to Flint's defence in the hope that he'd forget that Darwin might be behind his arrest.

'Mr Beastwood isn't making it up,' he said. 'Lydia is my wife and Phyllis is my neighbour. They took Uncle Loops to hospital in my wheelbarrow.'

The arresting officers looked very disappointed. They had been after Beastwood for years and it looked as if he was about to get away with murder yet again.

'We can still bang him to rights, though, can't we, guv?' said the tall one.

'The footprint is bound to stand up in court,' said the short one.

The constable behind the desk put his hand up and coughed politely.

'About that footprint,' he said. 'It's just a hunch, but you don't suppose it's got anything to do with those fake feet Ozzi was waving about do you, sir?'

The detective, who was as keen as anyone to see Beastwood behind bars, thought for a second and shook his head.

'No. Stick to your desk job, lad – Flint's going down. Take him away, boys!'

'You can't hold me here – you have no evidence!' yelled Flint as they dragged him down to the cells.

'We'll find some,' said the detective. 'You can sleep easy now, Mr Stigson.'

But Maurice wasn't so sure. Flint had faced a jail sentence on many occasions but, somehow, he was always released without charge. Even more of a worry, when he arrived home, Darwin told him with great delight that yes, he *had* found the T. Rex footprint and called the police – hurrah!

'I'm afraid Flint Beastwood's innocent,' said Mr Stigson. 'If the police can't find any concrete evidence against him, they'll have to let him go.'

Darwin gulped.

'He's going to kill me, isn't he, Dad?'

Half an hour later, there was a loud knock at the door.

CHAPTER 6

OFFSIDE

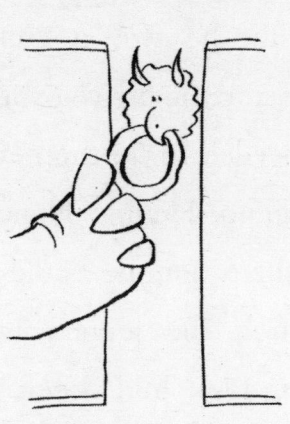

To Darwin's enormous relief, it wasn't Flint
Beastwood at the door – it was a bagaceratops
who had come to fix the window.

'Barry Stow!' he said, shaking Darwin by the
hand. 'All right, mate? Only you look like

you've seen a T. Rex or summink. Don't worry, I don't bite. Your dad came in the shop earlier and asked me to pop round. Sorry I'm a bit late – the puttersump went on me motor.'

The good news was that the bagaceratops was a completely harmless herbivore. The bad news was that he was a completely useless glazier. For a start, he arrived without any of the equipment needed to fix the new pane of glass he was carrying. Having leant it against the front step where anyone could fall over it, he peered through the jagged hole where the original window had been smashed and demanded refreshments.

'Is the wife in, pal?' he said. 'No? Stick the kettle on then, I'm gasping.'

'But you haven't done any work yet,' said Mr Stigson.

Barry Stow adjusted his glasses, which were

mended with sticky plaster.

'I have, as it happens,' he said. 'I've been sussing out the correct thickness of the glass required, putting it in me van and all sorts.'

He poked the window frame with his pencil and frowned.

'Oh dear, oh dear, oh dear,' he said. 'You're riddled with wet rot, mate. That's going to shove the price up a bit.'

'Really?' said Mr Stigson. 'The frames are metal. I didn't know metal could rot.'

'You'd be surprised,' said the glazier. 'Has the kettle boiled yet? I'll have a nice cup of splosh with six sugars, if it's no trouble.'

Mr Stigson had much better things to do than make tea. Even so, he made some in an old mug and handed it to the glazier, hoping that it would make him get a move on.

'Smashin',' said Barry, drinking it with a loud slurp. 'Bit wet without a biscuit, though, innit? Got any chocolate fingers?'

An hour later, he'd finished off all the biscuits but still hadn't started on the window.

'What's the hold-up?' asked Mr Stigson. 'I'd like it fixed today if possible.'

Barry sucked his teeth and looked shocked.

'*Today?* You'll be wanting the moon on a stick next. I can't start till my mate Mick gets here with the putty.'

'Why didn't you bring any putty?' asked Mr Stigson.

He was beginning to lose patience and, apart from that, Mrs Stigson wasn't going to be very happy if she came home to a broken window.

'It's a two-man job,' insisted Barry. 'Mick will be here in a minute.'

A minute passed. Then several minutes. Then an hour – and still the glazier's mate hadn't arrived. Darwin looked at the clock. It was getting late.

'Dad, I thought we were going to visit Uncle Loops in hospital,' he said. 'I'm really worried about him. If we don't go soon, visiting time will be over.'

Mr Stigson finished changing Shelly's nappy and took the peg off his nose.

'Let's just get our coats, take the bus and let the glazier get on with it,' he said. 'We could be stuck here all afternoon waiting for Mick and his putty to turn up.'

While he went upstairs to fill Uncle Loops's overnight bag with spare pyjamas, slippers and magazines, Darwin quickly made a get-well-soon card. He'd almost finished colouring it in when the doorbell rang again.

'That'll be Mick,' called Mr Stigson. 'Let him in, Darwin.'

But it wasn't the glazier's mate coming to fix the window. It was Flint the gangster coming to smash it again. And he wasn't alone. He had Mr Cretaceous and Terry O'Dactyl with him, both of whom were spoiling for a fight.

'Dad!' yelled Darwin.

Mr Stigson came running down the stairs with Shelly over his shoulder.

'Get out!' he shouted.

'Yes, I *did* get out,' said Flint triumphantly. 'And I shan't be going back inside. They haven't got a shred of evidence against me.'

'But what about the footprint?' said Darwin,

clapping his hands over his mouth the second he'd said it.

Flint chucked him under the chin with his scythe-like claw.

'You mean the one you found in your front garden and blabbed about to the police?' he said. 'Ozzi made it, not me. The plaster cast fitted his fake T. Rex feet perfectly.'

He looked at Shelly and licked his lips. 'I'm as innocent as . . . a babe in arms, aren't I, boys?'

'You are, boss,' said Mr Cretaceous, sniffing Shelly's toes. 'Oooh . . . imagine them braised with a bit of gravy, Terry.'

'Very tender, to be sure,' gibbered the pterodactyl, pecking at Darwin's hat. 'Much more tender than the brother.'

'I'll tenderise him!' said Mr Cretaceous, advancing on Darwin with his ham-sized fists up. Flint Beastwood held him back.

'No, no, Mr Cretaceous,' he said. 'Even if you beat him to a pulp, the boy will be completely inedible – do you know why? Because he tastes of GRASS!'

Terry O'Dactyl – who was a few peanuts short of a bird table – didn't quite get the joke. He put his skull-like head to one side and peered up at Flint.

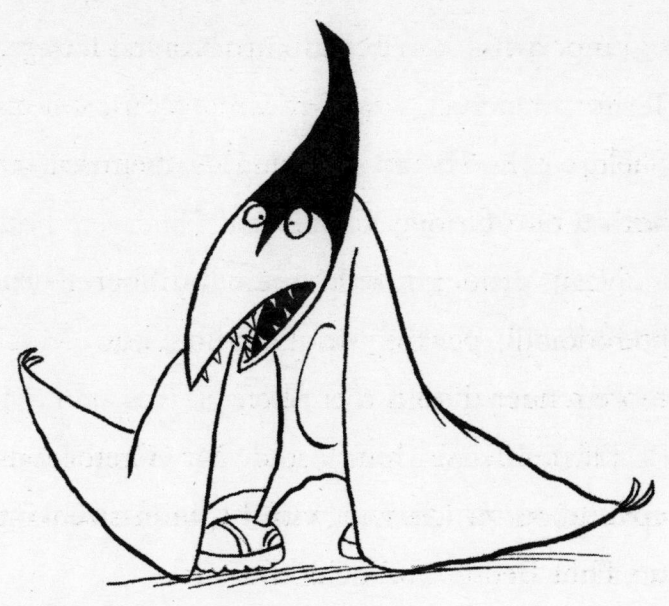

'Is a "grass" a little creep who tittle-tattles to the police about someone they think has done a terrible, awful thing, boss?'

Flint Beastwood nodded slowly.

'Correct, Mr O'Dactyl,' he said. 'And being carnivores, we hate grasses, don't we, lads? Remind me, what is it that we do to them?'

'We bite their heads off and use them as bowling balls,' said Mr Cretaceous.

'And awful terrible things besides,' tittered Terry O'Dactyl.

Darwin had heard enough. He was scared, but he was also furious. If Ozzi and Flint were both innocent, there was only one other suspect who had a motive for throwing that boulder.

'I'm sorry I told the police it was you, Mr Beastwood,' said Darwin. 'I was wrong. I was upset about Uncle Loops and I wasn't thinking straight.'

'There,' said Mr Stigson. 'Darwin's apologised. Let's forget it and have a nice cup of tea. I'd offer you a biscuit but —'

'Apology not accepted!' roared Flint. 'Your son must be punished.'

'Can I punish him now, boss?' pleaded Mr Cretaceous, gnashing his teeth.

'Oh, please, please, please!' wheedled Terry O'Dactyl, clattering his bony beak.

Flint Beastwood held one claw up.

'Excuse me? Why should you two have all the fun? Let's punish him together!'

Darwin folded his arms and, with great bravado, stood up to the gang who were stalking him round the hall table. 'The one who needs punishing is Rocky Beastwood!' he said. 'He broke our window because we wouldn't let him play football with us today.'

Flint looked at him, aghast. His face had turned purple with rage.

'Now you accuse my nephew?' he bellowed.

'He's a good boy. He wouldn't break wind, let alone a window. How dare you not let him play!'

'He stole my sister's doll,' said Darwin.

Mr Stigson hopped up and down nervously and grabbed Darwin by the hand.

'Let's leave it, shall we?' he said. 'Come along, let's go and visit Loops.'

Flint blocked the doorway and folded his tiny arms.

'You seem to be in rather a hurry to get to hospital,' he said. 'Maybe we can speed things up a bit, eh lads?'

'Yes, let's put them in hospital!' shrieked the mad pteranodon.

'*Fight!*' boomed Mr Cretaceous.

'Just as well I never fixed that broken window – waste of time,' said Barry as Beastwood sent Mr Stigson flying through it.

Just then, Mrs Stigson and Mrs Merrick came
back down the path.

'Oh my goodness!' gasped Mrs Stigson. 'Are
you all right, Maurice?'

Mr Stigson brushed himself down and, before she could stop him, grabbed the dustbin lid. Using it as a shield, he ran back indoors.

'It's all kicking off in there, ladies,' said Barry. 'Biff! Thump! Pow! I'd call the cops if I were you.'

But Mrs Merrick had a better idea.

'I'll go and rescue the children,' she said, whirling her handbag round her head. 'Lydia, you run round to Lou Gooby's and tell her your family is in mortal danger and to come here at once.'

Because of her huge size, the mamenchisaurus was the only herbivore Flint's gang were truly afraid of – it was worth a try.

'Hang on in there, son!' cried Mrs Stigson. 'Everything will be fine.'

But as Terry O'Dactyl dangled him from the ceiling fan and spun him around, Darwin found this very hard to believe.

CHAPTER 7

GAME ON!

Mrs Stigson ran all the way to Lou Gooby's, but it wasn't the steep hill that took her breath away – it was the sight of a small T. Rex sobbing on the mamenchisaurus's shoulder.

Lou was lying down, or he'd never have

reached – she was so huge, it looked as if he was clinging on to the side of a mountain.

'Ah, Missy Stigson,' Lou said in her gentle Chinese accent. 'You are looking most anxious.

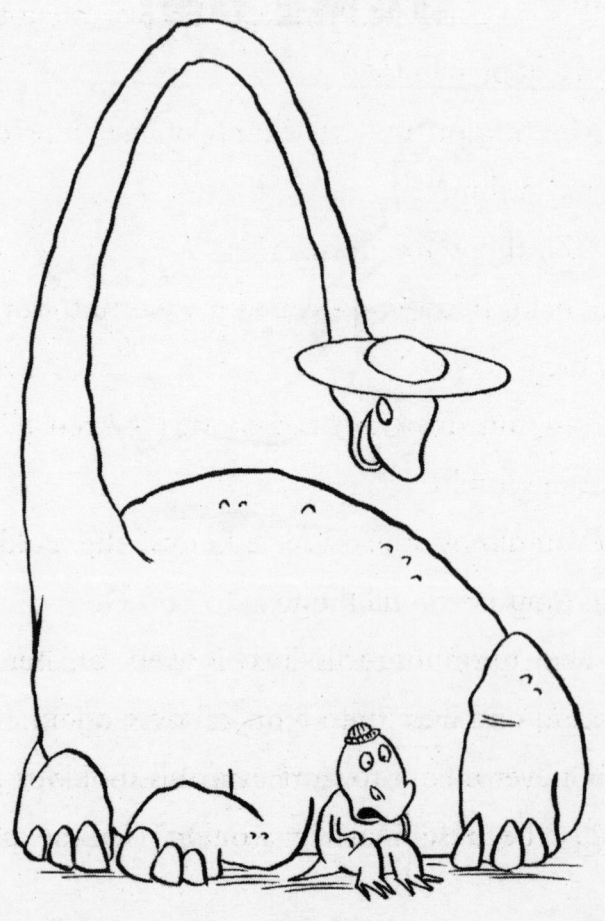

Do not be afraid of this young carnivore. He is more to be pitied than scolded.'

The little T. Rex gazed up at Mrs Stigson with watery eyes, his bottom lip quivering.

'I'm so sorr-eee,' he wept. 'I never meant to break your window.'

Mrs Stigson put her hands on her hips and glared at him.

'*You* threw the boulder?'

Rocky Beastwood wiped his snotty snout on his arm.

'No, my arms are too short. I kicked it,' he said miserably.

'You almost killed Uncle Loops!' she scolded. 'He may never walk again.'

The tyrannosaurus rex looked at her in dismay and burst into tears all over again.

'I never meant to hurt him, missus. I was just angry because Darwin wouldn't let me play football with him 'cause I stole his sister's doll.'

Lou Gooby patted his head.

'Master Beastwood must learn to deal with big anger and thieving issue,' she said. 'I blame the parents.'

'Ain't got none,' sniffed Rocky. 'Uncle Flint and Auntie Tara look after me now.'

'He come from broken home,' said Lou Gooby sympathetically.

Having spent the afternoon scooping Uncle Loops off the hospital floor after he'd fallen off his bedpan, Mrs Stigson wasn't in a very forgiving mood.

'I expect *he* broke it,' she said. 'I don't know why you're snivelling, Rocky. Your uncle is smashing up my house and trying to kill my husband and children as we speak.'

Lou Gooby's eyebrows shot up in alarm.

'Why you not say earlier? Come, we have no time to lose or big blood barf!'

Lou raised herself up onto her thunderous thighs. As the ground trembled beneath her and trees were trampled underfoot, Mrs Stigson and Rocky followed her back to Fossil Street.

When they arrived, the scene before them was not a happy one – the door was hanging off, all the windows were broken and the fight had spilt out into the front garden. Even the glazier and his mate had joined in; there was putty everywhere.

'My roses!' wailed Mrs Stigson. 'They're ruined.'

Mrs Merrick was sitting on Mr Cretaceous and had him in a headlock by the bins. Darwin had managed to get down from the ceiling fan and was staggering dizzily across the lawn, trying to lasso Terry O'Dactyl with the washing line. Shelly was crawling on the roof and Mr Stigson

was running away from Flint Beastwood, who had turned the hosepipe on him.

'Don't worry, Lydia. I've got everything under control,' he said.

'Honestly, Maurice,' said Mrs Stigson. 'I asked you to do one simple little thing . . .'

'STOOOOOOOOP!' bellowed Lou Gooby.

The carnivores froze in terror; Flint's hosepipe went limp – *nobody* messed with the mamenchisaurus. She waited for complete silence with her feet pressed together in a yoga pose, then spoke.

'Mr Beastiewood, your nephew has big fat confession to make,' she said, encouraging Rocky to come out from hiding behind her enormous backside. His knees had turned to jelly and it took him some time to wobble nervously over to Flint.

'I'm sorry, Uncle Flint,' he said, hanging his head. 'I done a most terrible thing.'

'Two terrible things, actually,' said Mrs Stigson.

Rocky counted his crimes on his claws and nodded.

'First I stole a dolly,' he said, the tears rolling down his scaly cheeks.

Flint shook his massive head in despair. 'I don't believe it!' he roared. 'Then what did you do?'

'Th-then I kicked a boulder through the window and almost killed Uncle Loops. I didn't mean to, Mr and Mrs Stigson. I'm soooooo sorry.'

Flint Beastwood struggled to control his rage. He put his hands around his nephew's throat and almost strangled him. But despite

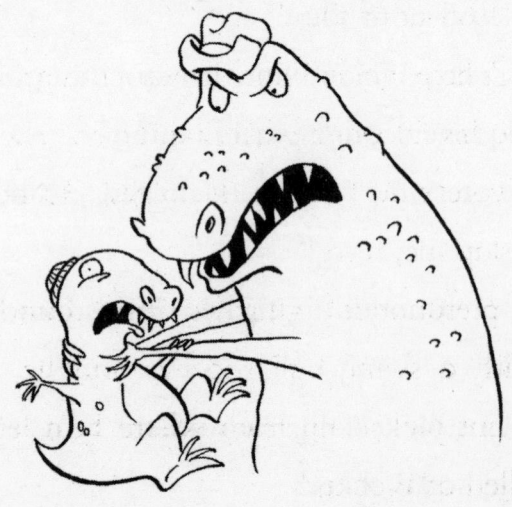

everything, the boy was *family* and his wife, Tara, was very attached to the little fellow. She'd kill anyone who hurt Rocky, even him.

'Don't be angry with me, Uncle Flint,' pleaded Rocky.

'Angry?' he screeched. 'I'm *furious*! Firstly, you play with dolls . . .'

There was a loud snigger in the corner and he swung round.

'Stop laughing, Mr Cretaceous, or I will wipe the smile off your face.'

'I can't help it, boss.' The deinosuchus grinned, clutching his sides and wheezing. 'Hee . . . hee . . . A carnivore who plays with dollies! Ha ha . . . Quick, slap me, Terry!'

The pteranodon whacked him round the face with a swing-ball racquet and he went quiet. Flint picked up from where he'd left off and yelled at Rocky.

'I've been like a father to you since I ate yours, and this is how you repay me? Not only do you play with dolls, you almost killed Uncle Loops! What do you have to say for yourself?'

'I'm sorry,' said Rocky.

'I should think so too!' growled Flint. 'You shouldn't have *almost* killed him! You should have killed him properly. It's that kind of thoughtless behaviour that gives carnivores a bad name.'

'Rocky Beastwood is a little goody two-shoes!' taunted Terry O'Dactyl.

'I said I'm sorry, Uncle,' whined Rocky.

Flint remained unmoved.

'That's another thing,' he said. 'How dare you apologise for knobbling a herbivore? Anyone would think you were glad Uncle Loops is alive. Go away and don't come back until you have his head on a plate – you disgust me.'

Darwin's dander was up – he strode over to Rocky and prodded him on the nose.

'Don't you go anywhere near my Uncle Loops or you'll have me to answer to!'

Seeing things were about to get out of hand, Lou Gooby put her foot down. It almost started

an earthquake and Mr Stigson was worried his house might collapse – there was not much of it left up after the battle – but at least Lou had everyone's full attention again.

'Now is time for carnivores and herbivores to make peace,' she said.

'Boring,' muttered Mr Cretaceous.

Lou Gooby blinked at him slowly, until he shrivelled and stopped being silly.

'Mr Flint, you take micky out of nephew for saying sorry, but it takes enormous guts.'

'Enormous guts?' frowned Mrs Merrick, sucking her massive stomach in. 'Is she talking about me?'

'No, Phyllis,' said Mrs Stigson, holding out her arms as the mastodon lifted Shelly down from the roof with her trunk. 'She's saying it's big of Rocky to apologise.'

'"Sorry" won't help Uncle Loops to walk!' shouted Mrs Merrick.

Lou Gooby nodded in agreement.

'Missy Phyllis make very good point. Peace Plan must bring Uptown and Downtown

Dinosaurs together to help aged uncle. You will all play in charity football match to raise money for mobility scooter for Unky Loops.'

'Brilliant idea!' whooped the Stigsons.

But Flint refused to play ball.

'A charity game to help a *herbivore*?' he spat. 'Over my dead body!'

Mr Cretaceous and Terry O'Dactyl exchanged disappointed glances and took him to one side.

'Don't be too hasty, boss,' said Mr C, lowering his voice to a menacing hiss. 'Do the maths – there are eleven players in each football team, which will give us the perfect opportunity to give eleven herbivores a proper kicking.'

'In front of all their fans!' tittered Terry O'Dactyl.

Beastwood thought about it for a moment, then his mouth stretched into a ghastly grin that showed all his pointy fangs.

'We'll destroy them,' he muttered under his breath. 'Any red-blooded carnivore would pay good money to see that.'

Mr Cretaceous nudged him in the ribs and whispered in his ear. 'We could charge them over the top for the tickets and pocket the difference.'

It was a no-brainer. Flint Beastwood walked over to the Stigsons and punched the air.

'GAME ON!' he roared.

CHAPTER 8

TOP SIGNING

The date for the charity football match was fixed. Having picked up lots of tips on the beautiful game during the World Cup, Mr Stigson appointed himself manager of the Uptown Herbivores. So far, the only players he'd signed apart from himself were Darwin, Mrs Merrick and Sir Tempest; it was hardly a dream team. To make matters worse, they were all sitting in his front room, moaning.

'We're seven players short, Dad,' said Darwin. 'And that's without any substitutes. Can't you put Mum in goal?'

'Don't even think about it, Maurice,' said Mrs Stigson. 'I'm too busy looking after Shelly and running back and forth to the hospital to visit Uncle Loops.'

'How is dear Augustus?' said Sir Tempest. 'Is he on the mend?'

'Round the bend,' scoffed Mrs Merrick. 'They couldn't find his brain when they X-rayed his head.'

'Maybe there was something wrong with the machine,' said Darwin.

In his experience, Uncle Loops was cleverer than he let on. His brain might have shrunk over the years, but he never forgot the important things, like the words to rude songs, Darwin's birthday and where the sweet tin was kept.

'I've been thinking . . .' said Sir Tempest.

'That's never good,' mumbled Mrs Merrick. 'Unless you're thinking of passing the biscuits.'

The triceratops handed her the plate of custard creams and continued.

'I'm not happy with our team name,' he said. 'Whoever thought of Uptown Herbivores should be fired.'

'It was me,' said Mr Stigson. 'What's wrong with it?'

'It lacks drama,' said Sir Tempest, beating his

teacup loudly with the sugar spoon. 'Dull! Dull! Dull! I think we should call ourselves the Fabulous Footy Fandangos.'

The rest of
the team gazed
up at the
ceiling and
tried not to
laugh. Thinking
that maybe
they just hadn't
heard him,
Sir Tempest

stood up, did a twirl and said it again.

'Now let's hear it for . . . the Fabulous Footy
Fandangos!'

There was an embarrassed silence which
seemed to last for about an hour.

'Let's not,' said Mrs Merrick. 'It makes us
sound like a ditsy dance troop.'

Sir Tempest pursed his leathery lips and put
his three horns in the air.

'So I'm ballet-trained,' he sulked. 'At least I'm light on my feet – which is more than can be said of you, Phyllis. If you eat any more biscuits we could use you as the ball.'

They glared at each other from opposite ends of the sofa. Caught in the crossfire of bad feeling, Darwin tried to distract them.

'How about calling ourselves the Fossil Street Footers?' he said.

'I like it,' said his mother. 'Let's vote. Who wants Fabulous Footy Fandangos?'

Sir Tempest held up all four feet. 'Cheat!' said Mrs Merrick, whacking him with a cushion.

'Who's in favour of Fossil Street Footers?' said Mr Stigson.

'Me!' said Mrs Merrick, holding up her trunk.

All the Stigsons voted for it and, as they outnumbered even Sir Tempest's four feet, the name was adopted. Now all Mr Stigson had to do was sort out the far trickier problem of finding more players. He had no relatives to call on, as they had all been eaten by carnivores, apart from Uncle Loops. And as he couldn't even stand up, it was pointless asking him.

'Leave it to me, Dad,' said Darwin. 'Frank and Ernest will want to be in the team and I can always ask Dippy Egg. Maybe his friends could play too.'

'Is that gawky gallimimus still sharing a cave with a load of catering students?' asked Mrs Merrick.

'As far as I know,' said Darwin.

'Good,' she said. 'Ask them to cook me a take-away.'

While his father worked on a game strategy that played to the strengths of a less-than-nimble mastodon and a more-than-clumsy triceratops, Darwin set off to the Primeval Forest to look for his old mate Dippy. His mother left him strict instructions not to go deep into the woods, but as usual he ignored it – it was broad daylight. He'd be fine.

In many ways, it was safer knowing that Ozzi was still locked in a police cell. If Darwin saw raptor footprints or heard a scary roar, at least he'd know it was a real carnivore instead of the australopithecus playing tricks, and he could run like the wind.

As it turned out, all the carnivores were at home watching the big match – Velociraptor

Victors versus Mosasaurus Almighty — so he had nothing to fear. The worst thing that happened was that Nogs found him and wouldn't go away. He was missing Ozzi and wanted to play, and when Darwin refused to

throw his stick for him, the cynognathus knocked him over, sat on his chest and licked his face. Apart from having terrible dog breath,

Nogs was so heavy Darwin couldn't push him off, so he was very grateful when he heard a familiar voice.

'Heeeeey, Darwin! Long time no see, matey,' said Dippy, picking up the stick Nogs had dropped and hurling it as far as he could.

'Good doggy, fetch!' he said.

Nogs shot after it and Darwin sat up and wrung the slobber out of his hat. 'Thanks, Dippy.'

The gallimimus helped him up.

'One good turn deserves another.' He smiled. 'If you hadn't taught me to read that time Beastwood kidnapped you, I'd still be his slave. As it is, I've passed my catering exams and I'm thinking of starting my own restaurant.'

'Fantastic,' said Darwin. 'Mrs Merrick will be pleased. But I haven't just come to say hello. There's a charity football match – we're short of players and I wondered if you'd be on our side?'

Dippy put a friendly arm around him.

'I'll always be on your side,' he said. 'Count me in. Is it a friendly game?'

Darwin pulled a face. 'Carnivores versus herbivores.'

Dippy looked at him in disbelief.

'You're joking. That's not a game, that's a war.'

'It's to prevent a war,' said Darwin. 'It was Lou Gooby's idea. It's a long story.'

'I like long stories,' said Dippy. 'Tell me all about it on the way to mine.'

By the time Darwin reached Dippy's cave, he'd filled him in on all the details about Rocky Beastwood kicking the boulder that hit Uncle Loops and about the fake footprint and the terrible fight that followed between Flint's gang and his family.

'The carnivores will never change,' said Dippy. 'All we can hope is that one day they'll be extinct, but I can't see it happening.'

'Me neither,' said Darwin.

'Cheese and fungus omelette?' asked Dippy as they went inside. 'Get another plate out,' he

called to his
cave-mate, 'we've
got a guest.'

A therizinosaurus
appeared, wearing
an apron which
was far too
small for
him and
waving a
frying pan.
Darwin
recognised him
immediately –
Uncle Loops had found him in the garden last
year, crying for his parents after Flint had made
him an orphan. He and Darwin had become
good friends, but they hadn't seen each other
for ages.

'Graham!' Darwin said. 'Great to see you! What are you doing here?'

'We're cave-sharing,' explained Dippy. 'My college-mates who lived here left and got jobs. I was rattling around on my own, Graham had nowhere to live – sorted!'

'Sorted,' laughed Graham, tossing an egg in the air and catching it in the pan.

Darwin looked at the gentle omnivore and smiled. He'd forgotten how huge his hands were – bigger than any carnivore's. It would be hard to kick a ball past those.

'You don't fancy going in goal, do you?' he said, smiling.

After a delicious omelette, Darwin had signed up Graham and Dippy, who promised to get in touch with his old cave-mates and persuade them to play in the charity match too. Fossil Street Footers were still one man down, but it was Darwin's lucky day.

As he waved goodbye to his friends on the edge of the forest and made his way across No Man's Land, he saw a crowd of little herbivores waving their autograph books excitedly at a familiar figure sitting on the bench. Darwin could hardly believe his eyes. It was a titanosaurus, but not just any old titanosaurus – it was Rabid Deckham, the world famous footballer! He was well-known for his charity work – but would he be willing to play for Fossil Street Footers?

There was no harm in asking.

CHAPTER 9

STUFFED!

To Darwin's amazement, Rabid Deckham signed up for Fossil Street Footers on the spot. He took very little persuading, saying that it had to be better than the team he was playing for at the moment, and agreed to be their centre forward.

Darwin was so thrilled, he skipped all the way home. With Deckham on their side, the herbivores were surely guaranteed a victory over the carnivores. His speed and fancy footwork were legendary. Darwin couldn't wait to see the look on his dad's face when he told him.

'Dad? Dad!' he whooped. 'You'll never guess what!'

But to his dismay, his father wasn't the least bit impressed when he told him. In fact, he looked rather annoyed.

'I don't care who he is,' he said. 'He's not playing centre forward.'

'Why not?' said Darwin.

'Because *I* am,' said Mr Stigson.

Like many stegosaurs, Maurice had dreamt of being a professional footballer since he was an egg. He had high hopes of being man of the match at the charity game and he didn't want

Deckham stealing his glory.

'But Rabid Deckham is invincible!' said Darwin. 'When did you last play, Dad?'

Mr Stigson hadn't actually kicked a ball for at least five years. Mrs Stigson had made him hang up his boots because he had a dodgy knee, but he wasn't about to admit it.

'It's like riding a bike, son,' he said. 'You never forget how to do it.'

'You can't ride a bike,' said Darwin. 'The last time you tried, you fell off.'

It was a fair point, but his father refused to discuss the matter any further.

'I'm the manager,' he said, 'and I'm playing centre forward. We're having a practice in the park on Sunday. I've told Mrs Merrick and Sir Tempest to meet us there and I'd be grateful if you'd tell the rest of the team – including Rabid Wotsitsname – to arrive at nine o'clock sharp.'

'Deckham's got an international game that day,' said Darwin. 'I'm not sure he'll be able to make football practice in the kid's playground.'

Mr Stigson tutted out loud. 'His loss,' he said. 'I'll just have to knock him into shape nearer the time.'

Sunday arrived. Darwin had cleaned his boots and was about to call for Frank and Ernest when his dad sprinted downstairs in his kit.

'You can't go out in those shorts, Maurice,' giggled Mrs Stigson. 'They're far too tight. It'll put Mrs Merrick off her game.'

'Nonsense,' said Mr Stigson, tweaking the crotch. 'They make me look the part.'

'I can see your parts from here,' said Mrs Stigson.

Not wishing to be seen with his dad, Darwin ran ahead and knocked for the twins. But if he thought his dad's kit was embarrassing, it was nothing compared to Sir Tempest's. When they arrived at No Man's Land, he was posing in a tiny pair of Speedos, flippers and a snorkel.

'Why on earth are you dressed like that,

Stratford?' said
Mr Stigson,
puffing from
the rear.

'You said
I'll have to
dive for the
ball, Maurice,'
said Sir
Tempest.

Mr Stigson
put his head
in his hands and wailed.

'Yes – in goal! *Not* at the seaside. What were
you thinking of?'

Darwin was more concerned about what his
father was thinking of, playing Sir Tempest in
that position – he couldn't see him jumping to
save the ball.

'Put Graham in goal, Dad,' he said, pointing as the therizinosaurus came ambling over with Dippy and friends. 'Look at the claws on him! He'd be brilliant.'

Mr Stigson shook his head.

'No, it'll ruin my strategy,' he said, whipping out a piece of paper. 'I've drawn it all up now and I haven't got a rubber to change it – where's Mrs Merrick?'

'At a cake sale,' said Sir Tempest. 'Why?'

'I want her on the wing.'

'She hasn't got any wings,' said Sir Tempest. 'But I could lend her my pair from when I played a fairy in *A Midsummer Night's Scream*. The audience loved my Bottom.'

Darwin threw up his hands in despair as Mrs Merrick came into view, stopping every few seconds to eat another doughnut.

'You can't put Mrs Merrick on the wing,

Dad. Wingers have to be fast.'

'He's right,' said Sir Tempest. 'Phyllis will need a taxi to get anywhere near the ball. You're a rubbish manager, Maurice. Put Dippy on the wing.'

Sick of everyone giving him advice, Mr Stigson peeped his whistle to shut them up. The referee on match day was going to be Boris the Mayor but, meanwhile, he stepped into his shoes.

'I know what I'm doing,' he said, waving his game plan at them. 'Do as you're told and get into your positions or I'll send you off. Phyllis, stop laughing at my shorts and keep your eye on the ball.'

'I *am*, Maurice,' groaned Mrs Merrick. 'Get on with it.'

Unfortunately, as Mr Stigson kicked it into play, the ball binked off Sir Tempest's snorkel and landed in Mrs Merrick's open handbag.

There was an ugly moment where she tipped it upside down and her lipstick, keys and spare doughnuts fell onto the pitch. As she bent over to pick them up, Dippy skidded into her and swept her feet away.

'Foul!' cried Mrs Merrick, waving her legs in the air.

'It is from where I'm standing,' winced Sir Tempest.

Two minutes into practice time and the game had already fallen into chaos. It didn't say much about Mr Stigson's managing skills or his players, so it was just as well he didn't realise the Fossil Street Footers were being watched – Flint Beastwood had sent his henchmen to spy on them. Right now, they were hiding behind the kids' roundabout and, as the Footers' game went from bad to worse, the carnivores kept up a running commentary.

'That triceratops has four left feet,' squeaked Terry O'Dactyl. 'He's let in every goal so far, so he has – and what's the mastodon doing on the wing?'

'Having a lie-down by the looks of it.' Mr Cretaceous grinned. 'That little steggie, Darwin, would be one to watch, but he's got no one to pass to – their idiot manager isn't playing his gallimimus to his best advantage – and they've only got ten men.'

'Really? I can't count that far, I only have two fingers,' said the pteranodon. 'Raptor Road Rovers will wipe the grass with them, won't we?'

'We'll crush the veggies underfoot,' said Mr Cretaceous gleefully, stamping his feet and creating huge craters in the tarmac to demonstrate how much damage he could do.

They were about to sneak back to Beastwood's headquarters to tell Flint the great news when another player turned up on the pitch. He kicked his tracky bottoms off, rolled up his sleeves to expose his tattoos and apologised to Mr Stigson.

'Sorry I'm late, boss. I was playing for Milan and we went into overtime.'

He quickly warmed up, then grabbed the

ball that Mrs
Merrick had
just booted
offside with
his left foot,
did some
amazing
tricks with
it, then
raced down
the pitch,
nipping in
and out of
the defence

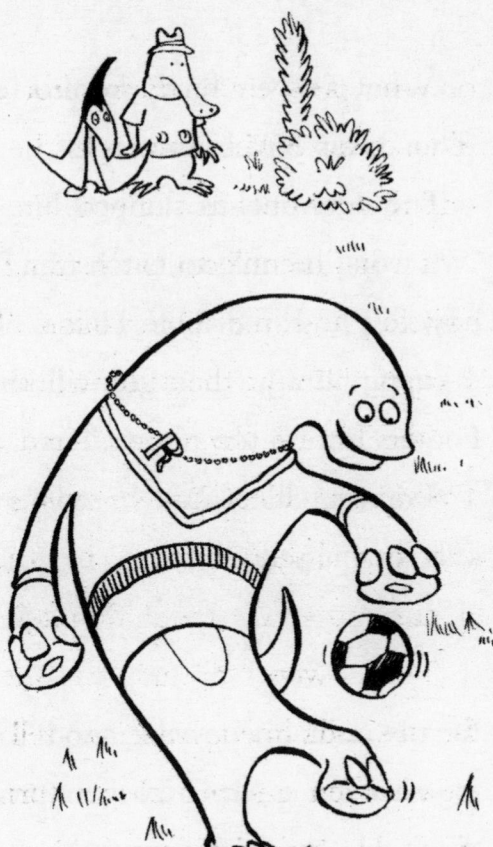

with breathtaking skill and determination.

'Oh, bogswamp!' swore Mr Cretaceous. 'It's Rabid Deckham. What's he doing here? We won't stand a chance if he's playing for the herbivores.'

'What if we eat him?' drooled Terry O'Dactyl. 'That'd stop him in his tracks.'

The deinosuchus slapped him on the beak. 'We won't be able to catch him,' he said. 'Look how fast he can dribble. Flint is not going to be a happy bunny when you tell him Fossil Street Footers have a top player, Terry.'

'I'm not telling him!' hissed Terry. 'He always kills the messenger.'

In the end, they held hands and told Flint together. Just as Mr Cretaceous predicted, the boss didn't take the news very well.

'*Deckham?*' he screamed, stubbing his cigar out on Terry's hat. 'Why didn't you two clowns sign him? If we lose this charity match, it will be your fault!'

He picked up his desk and threw it out of the

window, which happened to be shut at the time. He was just about to throw Mr Cretaceous after it when his wife, Tara, came in.

'Calm down, babe, that was a new desk,' she said. 'What's up? Lost at cards again?'

He broke a chair over Mr Cretaceous's head and explained.

'So?' Tara shrugged. 'Just 'cause they've got Deckham don't mean we have to lose.'

Flint Beastwood lowered himself into the chair he'd just broken and sat down hard on the floor.

'How can we possibly win?' he said. 'Deckham's a genius.'

'By doing what you do best, Beastie,' she said. 'You cheat.'

Flint Beastwood nodded slowly to himself.

'I'm good at cheating, aren't I?'

Then his face fell.

'But am I good enough? Cheating won't cut

it on its own. We need jiggery-pokery to beat them. We need skullduggery and trickery!'

'We need Ozzi,' said Tara.

A wicked smile spread over Flint's face.

'We do!' he said. 'I'll bail him out of jail and make him an offer he can't refuse. Either he helps me knobble the Flint Street Footers or I'll eat him. Ozzi owes me a big favour after making those T. Rex footprints. He almost put me in prison.'

'Go, Beastie! Go, Beastie!' sang Tara, flinging her scaly limbs about like a carnivorous cheerleader.

Flint filled a suitcase with fake banknotes to bribe Ozzi's jailer and commanded Mr Cretaceous to drive him to the police station. Shortly afterwards, the australopithecus was released back into the wild. As he didn't fancy being eaten, he agreed to Flint's demands and was driven back to The Prehysterical where he came up with a brilliant cheating-at-football strategy for Raptor Road Rovers.

Darwin didn't know it yet, but it looked like the herbivores were stuffed.

CHAPTER 10

RESULT!

The day of the charity match arrived and, to Darwin's joy, Uncle Loops was out of hospital. Although he was in a wheelchair, he was well enough to watch the game and was looking forward to it enormously.

'I should thank Ricky Boastwood for hitting me on the head,' he said as Mrs Stigson pushed him to the front of the packed stadium. 'If it hadn't been for him, I wouldn't be sitting here now, would I, Lorna?'

'I'm Lydia,' said Mrs Stigson.

Uncle Loops sighed.

'Your mother's changed her name again, Smelly,' he said to Darwin's baby sister as she sat in his lap, waving a football rattle.

'She's Shelly, not smelly,' said Mrs Stigson patiently.

Uncle Loops wrinkled his already wrinkly nose.

'She's both,' he said, holding her at arm's-length.

It was a shame Mrs Stigson had to go and change Shelly's nappy because she missed the Fossil Street Footers' grand entrance through

the tunnel. Mr Stigson was at the front, followed by Darwin carrying the team mascot – Uncle Loops's prehistoric teddy. 'Boo!' shouted the carnivore fans.

But as Mr Stigson jogged through the arch, the boos turned to hoorays when his head clanked against a cunningly-disguised bucket of stinking swamp water suspended over the tunnel exit. To the delight of the rowdy Raptor Road fans, it tipped all over him.

'Ozzi, Ozzi, Ozzi! Oi! Oi! Oi!' they chanted.

Mr Stigson let out a shriek and started rummaging in his shorts. Darwin didn't know where to look.

'Dad, don't do that in public! You're so embarrassing.'

'I've got a frog down my pants!' panicked Mr Stigson, pulling his shorts down.

'Shall I help you get it out, Maurice?' said Sir Tempest.

Luckily the frog got out by itself, Mr Stigson pulled his shorts up and, with as much dignity as possible having just shown his undies to a crowd of fifty thousand, he led his team onto the pitch.

The herbivore fans clapped politely and shouted words of encouragement and, for a moment, the Footers were filled with confidence – but it was very short-lived. As Flint led Raptor Road Rovers out of the tunnel, their horrible hairy mascot slipped the lead Ozzi was holding, sprinted over to Darwin, snatched the teddy bear and romped off with it.

'No, Nogs! *Off!*' shouted the referee, Boris the Mayor.

He leapt up from the bench and blew his whistle. Within seconds, his face went a funny shade of scarlet. He clutched at his throat as his lips blew up like a puffer fish – someone had dipped his whistle in pepper. Choking and spluttering, he chased after the cynognathus but he was sliding about as if he'd hit black ice, and little wonder! As Boris went Arsenal over tip, he realised that someone had buttered his boots. By the time he'd wiped them clean on his hanky, Nogs had swallowed the teddy and had stuffing all round his face.

'One–nil!' roared the carnivores.

Mr Stigson had given his team a pep talk before they came on, but now Ozzi was back on the scene all his advice went out of the window – along with Flint's desk. Now it was every Footer for himself – or herself, in Mrs Merrick's case.

'Don't let that australopithecus make a monkey out of you, Maurice!' she said as the ref tossed the coin to start the game. Flint Beastwood pocketed it, then nutmegged the ball through Mr Stigson's legs to Terry O'Dactyl, who caught it in his beak and flew off with it.

Sir Tempest went over to the ref, tapped him on the shoulder and pointed at the sky. 'Excuse me, ref. The ball's gone out.'

'Has it?' whined Boris. 'I can't see a thing – I have pepper in my eyes.'

Sir Tempest put his hands on his hips, sauntered back onto the pitch and chatted to Mrs Merrick, who was sucking the filling out of a cream horn on the right wing.

'That's all we need, Phyllis,' he said. 'A blind ref.'

'I'm not sure it'll make any difference,' she

said. 'Run along now, Ozzi's about to throw the ball back on. Why don't you see if you can head it into the goal?'

Sir Tempest gazed at the cream horn longingly. 'Why don't you?' he said. 'You're not busy.'

'For heaven's sake, you two! Do I have to do everything?' muttered Mr Stigson, running down the pitch. 'Darwin, get ready for me to pass it to you. Hold on, where's Deckham?'

'He's stuck in the changing room,' said Darwin. 'Ozzi put superglue in his hairgel.'

'Cooee – I'm right behind you, Maurice!' said Sir Tempest as Ozzi threw the ball.

Mr Stigson missed the header and jumped back as it landed with a squelch on one of the triceratops's horns and spattered him with juice and pips.

'How curious,' said Sir Tempest. 'It tastes like a mouldy melon.'

'It *is* a
mouldy
melon,'
said Mrs
Merrick,
who'd
wandered
offside to

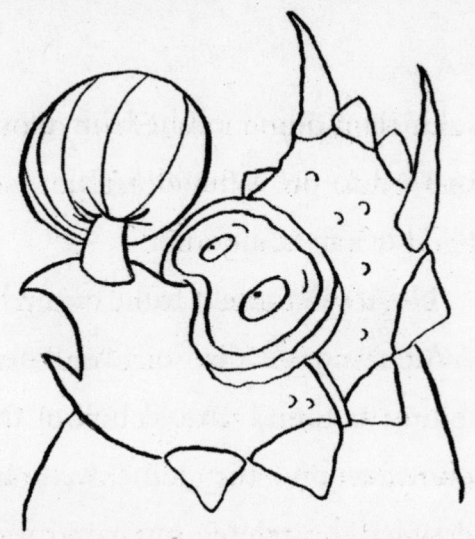

see what all the fuss was about. 'Don't keep it
all to yourself, Stratford, it's greedy.'

Meanwhile, Uncle Loops was struggling to
follow the game. He wasn't alone – Mrs Stigson
couldn't make head nor tail of it either.

'Why have they stopped, Laura?' he said.
'They tell me it's not over until the fat lady sings
and I haven't heard a tune out of Phyllis yet.'

'There's a problem with the ball,' said Mrs
Stigson. 'It looks as if it's been swapped for a
large, exotic fruit.'

Uncle Loops polished his glasses and leant forward to get a better look.

'That's nuts,' he said.

'No, it's definitely fruit,' argued Mrs Stigson.

After a great deal of fuss, Rabid Deckham's chauffeur found an old ball in the back of his limousine and the game went from worse to terrible. The referee lost control of the players and Nogs lost control of his bowels and committed more fouls on the pitch than the Raptor Road Rovers – as well as the stench, everybody kept stepping in it.

To add injury to insult, most of Flint's team were baryonyx who worked at the meat market. Being butchers, they were skilled hunters and as Deckham finally sorted his hair out and ran onto the pitch, they formed a pack, cornered him and trussed him up like an oven-ready chicken. It was just as well Mrs Merrick

had nail scissors in her handbag or he'd have
been tied up for the rest of the match.

The carnivores were three–nil up. As the
whistle went for halftime, the herbivores
limped back to their changing room, battered
and bruised.

'Do something, Dad,' said Darwin. 'The carnivores are walking all over us.'

Mr Stigson looked at the footmarks on his chest and asked himself the question he never wanted to ask: What would Deckham do? Finally, he turned to their star player.

'Any bright suggestions, Rabid?'

'From now on, we're going to have to play dirty,' said Deckham.

'I'm already filthy,' said Sir Tempest, rinsing his flippers in the shower and picking crazy foam out of his ears. 'How am I supposed to defend the goal when they keep squirting me?' he moaned.

Mrs Merrick filled the sink with water and sucked it up with her trunk.

'Squirt them back!' she said. 'I'll go in goal for the second half – Rovers won't know what's hit them. Deckham, organise the team into better positions, dear. We must go out there fighting!'

'Yes, boss. Nice one, Phyllis,' said Deckham.

'But *I'm* the boss,' said Mr Stigson pitifully.

'You've been demoted,' said Mrs Merrick. 'Get over it, Maurice.'

As much as he hated stepping down, as the Footers ran back onto the pitch with their heads held high and their custard pies held low, Mr Stigson soon saw sense.

Sick of being squirted by Mrs Merrick, the raptors waded about near the muddy goal and missed every time. At the other end, Deckham scored twice with the help of Dippy and his mates, but having been smothered in kisses by Sir Tempest, he didn't fancy scoring again. Happily, Frank chipped it to Ernest who booted it up the field to Darwin who struck it straight past Mr Cretaceous into the net.

'Goal!' whooped Mrs Stigson, leaping out of her seat. 'Well done, son!'

'What's the score, Lulu?' asked Loops as Boris blew his freshly washed whistle.

'Three all. It's a draw,' said Lydia. 'They're going to penalties.'

The Fossil Street Footers fans held their breath as Deckham got ready on the penalty spot and took the first shot. *Bang* – straight over the goalie's head! Frank and Ernest put in two belters, Darwin whammed one home and now it was Mr Stigson's turn.

'Good luck, Dad,' said Darwin.

Quietly confident, Mr Stigson ran up to the ball but just as he swung his leg back, someone lobbed a stink bomb from the stand and the ball hit the bar.

'Yoooooou're dead meat, hah!' screeched the Raptor fans.

'Who let that one go?' said Uncle Loops, wafting his tail. 'Was it me?'

'Not this time,' said Mrs Stigson. 'Shh, the Raptors are taking penalties now. If they put five in, they'll have won.'

Flint's side lined up, thumbing their noses cockily at the Fossil Street Footers. Mrs Merrick

braced herself in goal as O'Dactyl did a few trial run-ups. She was feeling peckish, and as he was dithering about, she fumbled in her bag for a packet of sherbet lemons.

'Goal!'

Terry had knocked one in.

Mrs Merrick concentrated, but as the next

player stepped forward, Ozzi poked her in the
bottom with her own hatpin. As she clutched
her buttocks,

the baryonyx took advantage and scored. Two
strikes later, the carnivores had equalised – they
only needed one more goal to win.

'Oh, no – Flint's put Rocky forward,' said
Mrs Stigson. 'He's their best striker. I remember
the damage he did to my window.'

'Go on, my son!' shouted Uncle Loops. 'On me head!'

Nobody knew why he said it – it made no sense at all – but it had a very bad effect on Flint's nephew. Seeing Loops in his wheelchair and knowing it was all his fault, he hesitated.

'Don't you dare muck this up, Rocky,' snarled Flint.

It was too late to change penalty-takers.

'Hurry up and shoot!' said Mrs Merrick. 'I want my dinner.'

Rocky's knees were trembling so badly he could hardly stand, but Uncle Flint was glaring at him, so he ran up and was just about to lose the match for Rovers when the whistle blew.

'Hold it!' shouted Boris. 'There's a streaker on the pitch!'

It was Flint's wife. Seeing that Rocky had no chance of getting the ball in the net, she had stripped off and was running round the pitch.

'Did he say there's a sneaker on the pitch?' said Uncle Loops.

'A *streaker*,' said Mrs Stigson. 'Do you need a new hearing aid?'

'New glasses!' said Loops.

'I don't know what she's up to,' said Mrs Stigson, 'but I bet it's a trick.'

To Mr Stigson's dismay, Mrs Stigson ran down the steps onto the field and whipped off her cardigan.

'Not you too, Lydia!' he said. 'What will the neighbours say?'

But Mrs Stigson had no intention of streaking. She chased after Tara, covered her with the cardigan and dragged her over to the sideline.

'Play on!' said Boris.

All eyes went back to Rocky. By now, he was in even more of a state. It was bad enough seeing the old stegosaur he'd put in a wheelchair without having to see Auntie Tara naked too. He put the ball on the penalty spot and looked up in disbelief. The goal seemed much closer than before – in fact, it was only a few centimetres away from his foot. It was impossible to miss.

'Ozzi shuffled it forward while everyone watched my missus, clever girl,' hissed Flint. 'He distracted the mastodon with a fairy cake. Quick, shoot before she notices!'

Rocky tapped the ball gently and, as Mrs Merrick was busy licking the icing off her ears, it rolled slowly past her into the back of the net.

'Goal!' whooped Flint. 'That's my boy!'

The carnivores went wild – even wilder than usual – Raptor Rovers had won! Darwin felt as sick as a parasaurolophus. But just as Mr Cretaceous was lifting Rocky onto his shoulders in triumph, the referee ran on with a tape measure.

'Nothing wrong with my eyes now,' he said. 'Someone has shifted the goalpost.'

He looked at his tape measure, which confirmed his suspicions.

'Just as I thought,' he said, reaching into his

pocket. He pulled out a wedge of red cards and waved them at all the Raptor Road Rovers.

'You cheated – the whole team is disqualified,' he announced.

'You can't send us all off – it was Ozzi!' roared Flint. 'I saw him!'

He was about to bite Boris's nose off when, suddenly, he stopped.

BOOM! BOOM! BOOM!

The ground shook beneath him and he fell to his knees.

'Do not argue with ref!' said Lou Gooby. 'You are bad loser, Mr Beastiewood. Fossil Street Footers *win*!'

The Fossil Street Footers fans tapped their tambourines in their excitement and, having done a lap of honour with his team, Darwin hurried over to see Uncle Loops.

'Why is everyone cheering, Daniel?' he said. 'Did the T. Rex strip off again?'

'We won!' whooped Darwin.

Uncle Loops leapt out of his wheelchair and did a victory dance.

'Yippee!' he shouted. 'Woo hoo! Up the Footers!'

Darwin looked at him in amazement. 'It's a miracle!' he cried. 'You can walk!'

Uncle Loops sat down quickly before anyone else noticed.

'Shhh,' he whispered. 'It wasn't the rock that did me in, it was Sir Compost's pea and ginger beer. I've been able to walk for ages . . . Promise not to tell anyone, Duncan.'

'I promise,' laughed Darwin. 'But why are you still pretending you can't walk?'

'I've always wanted one of those mobility scooters,' said Uncle Loops with a wink.

Darwin never told a soul. When all the cash from the charity match was counted, Augustus Loops was presented with the best scooter money could buy and lived the rest of his life in the fast lane, playing dodgems with Mrs Merrick.

Which could be why dinosaurs are now extinct.

THE UPTOWN AND DOWNTOWN PREHISTORIC SPOTTER'S GUIDE

DINOSAURS

Stegosaurus

(Steg-oh-saw-rus)

Example: The Stigsons

Triceratops

(Try-sair-a-tops)

Example: Sir Tempest

Ankylosaur

(Ank-ee-lo-saw)

Example: Frank and Ernest

Mamenchisaurus

(Mah-men-chee-saw-rus)

Example: Lou Gooby

Tyrannosaurus Rex

(Tie-ran-o-saw-rus Rex)

Example: Flint Beastwood

Gallimimus

(Gall-uh-my-mus)

Example: Dippy Egg

Therizinosaurus

(Ther-uh-zee-no-saw-rus)

Example: Graham

Titanosaurus
(Tie-tan-oh-saw-rus)
Example:
Rabid Deckham

Edmontonia
(Ed-mon-toe-nee-ah)
Example: Boris the Mayor

OTHER PREHISTORIC CREATURES

Deinosuchus
(Day-no-sook-us)
Example:
Mr Cretaceous

Pteranodon
(Tehr-ran-oh-don)
Example:
Terry O'Dactyl

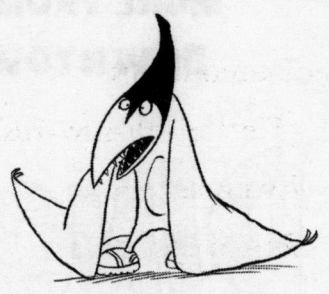

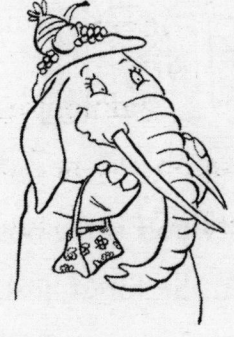

Mastodon
(Mas-toe-don)
Example: Mrs Merrick

Australopithecus
(Oss-tra-lo-pith-ah-cus)
Example: Ozzi

Cynognathus
(Sigh-nog-nay-thus)
Example: Nogs

DINOSAURS IN DISGUISE

T. Rex gangster Flint Beastwood is furious!
Dippy has gone missing in the forest, just
when Flint needed him to clean his toenails!

When Darwin the stegosaurus goes missing
too, the herbivores send out a search party.
But it's dangerous in the woods, with Flint's
deadly carnivore gang AND a scary new
dinosaur! So they come up with a brilliant
idea – to disguise themselves as trees . . .

DINOSAUR SCRAMBLE

When Mrs Stigson lays an egg there is great
rejoicing – Darwin has always wanted a
baby brother or sister to play with. But after
leaving it in the care of mad Uncle Loops,
Mrs Stigson is certain that something is
different. This is not her egg!

But whose egg is it, and what has happened?
And how will Darwin ever get the right one
back from gangster T. Rex, Flint Beastwood?

piccadillypress.co.uk/children

Go online to discover:

☆ more authors you'll love

☆ competitions

☆ sneak peeks inside books

☆ fun activities and downloads